Blue's Windy Day

Published by Advance Publishers, L.C.
www.advance-publishers.com

Written by K. Emily Hutta
Art layout by Niall Harding
Art composition by David Maxey
Produced by Bumpy Slide Books

ISBN: 1-57973-075-2

Blue's Clues Discovery Series

Wow, it sure is windy! Blue and I are excited because we've been waiting for a day like this to try out our new sailboat.

Hey! Would you like to sail our boat with us?
You would? Great!

It's sailing! Cool! Now it's sailing even faster!

Oh! I get it! The harder the wind blows, the faster our boat goes. Cool!

Let's see. What else can we do on a windy day? Yeah, we can watch the wind push the clouds across the sky. I love doing that. What about you, Blue? What do you want to do?

Oh! Great! We'll play Blue's Clues to figure it out.

Uh-oh, it looks like Shovel is having a little trouble building his sand castle with all of this wind.

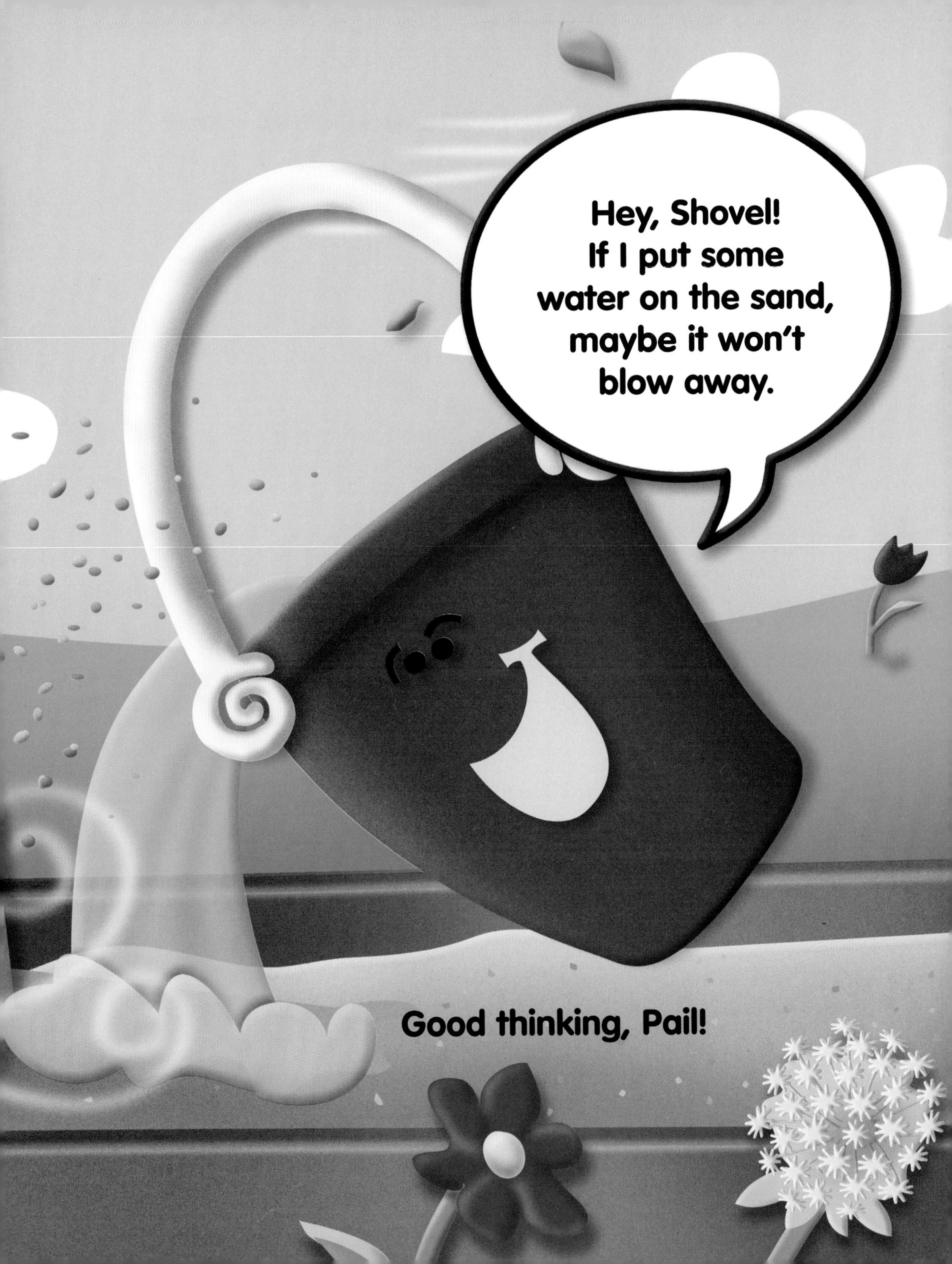

Good thinking, Pail!

The wind is blowing really strongly now!

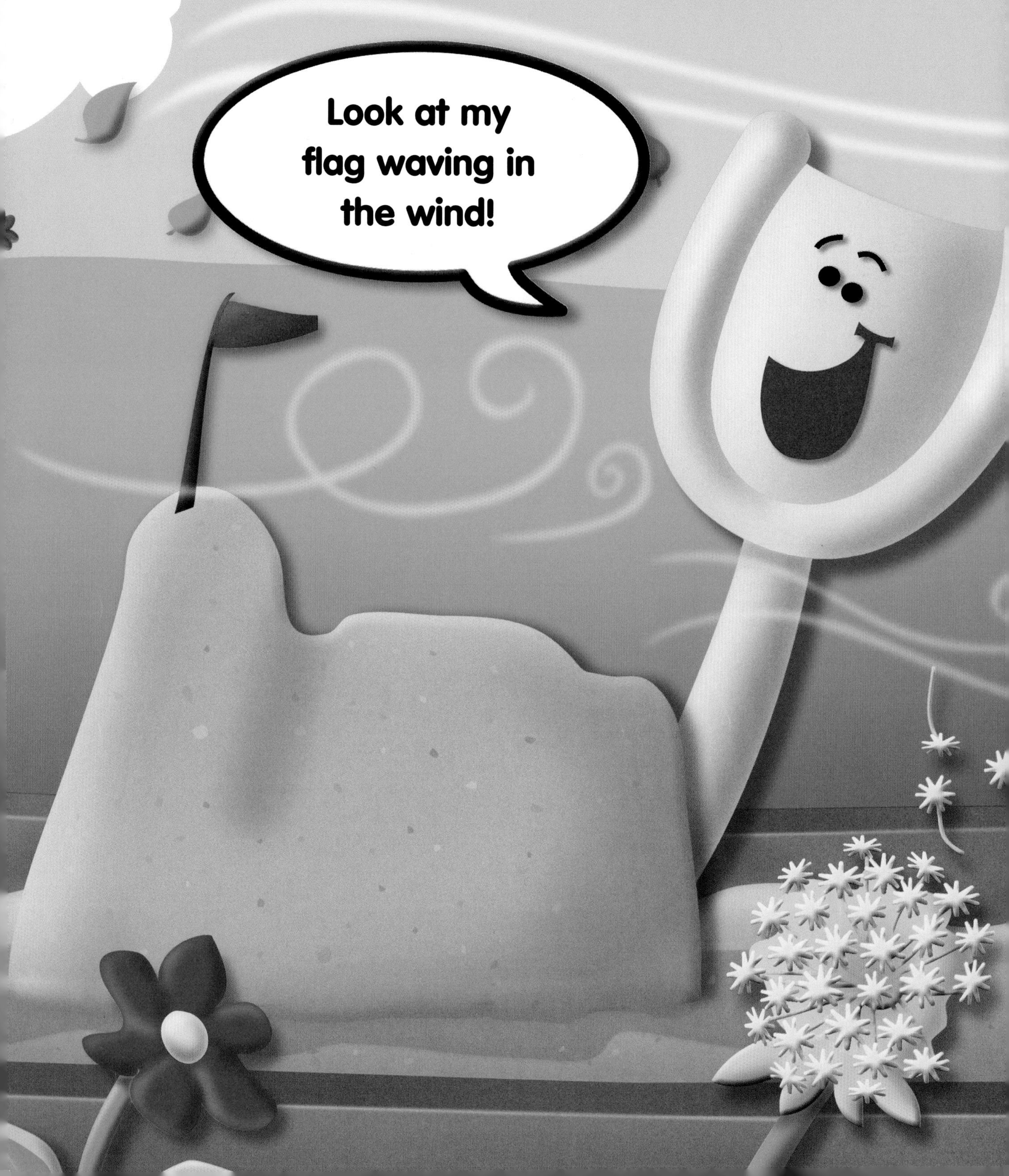

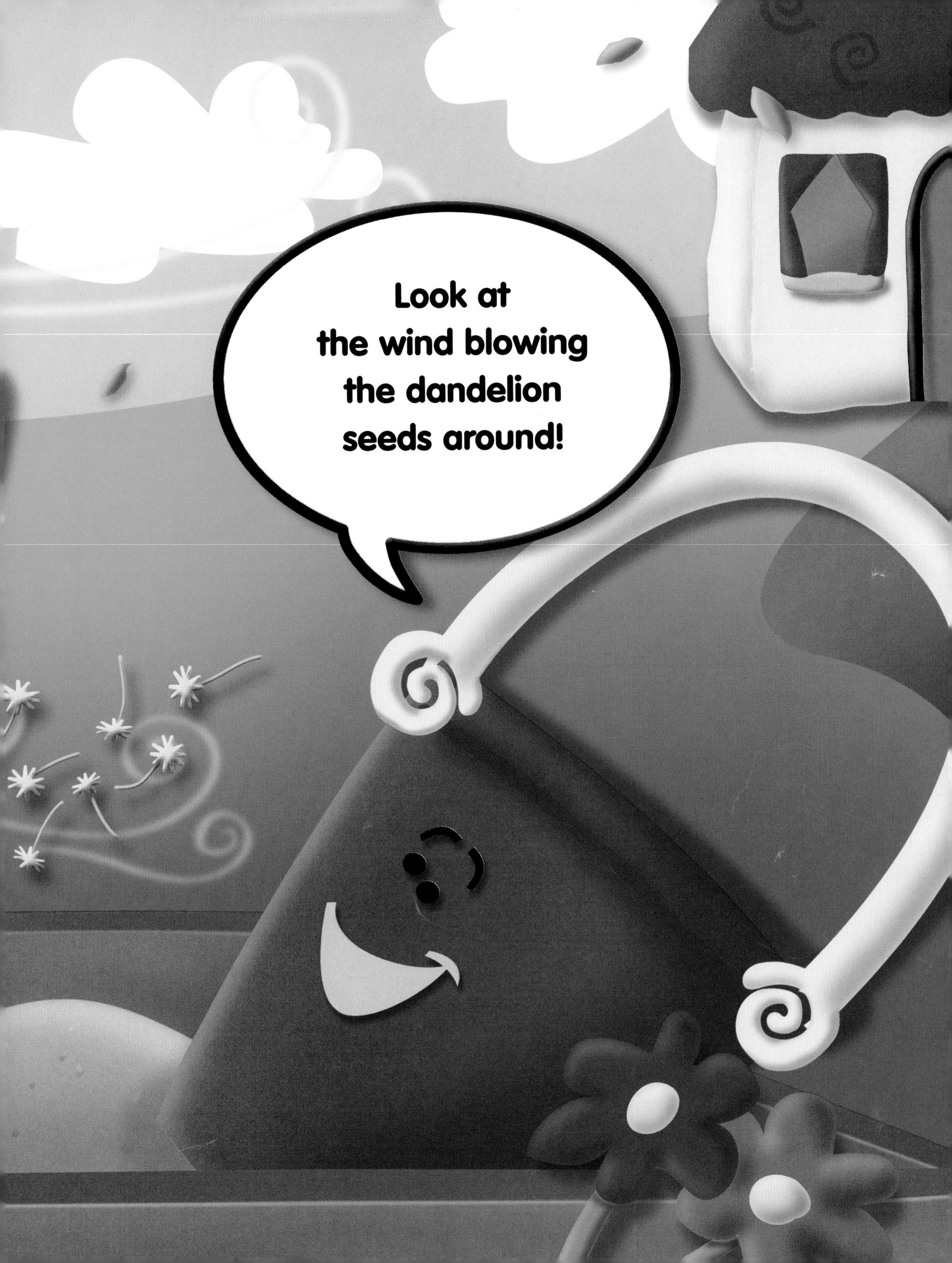
Look at the wind blowing the dandelion seeds around!

I thought I saw Blue come in here. What?
You see a clue? Where?

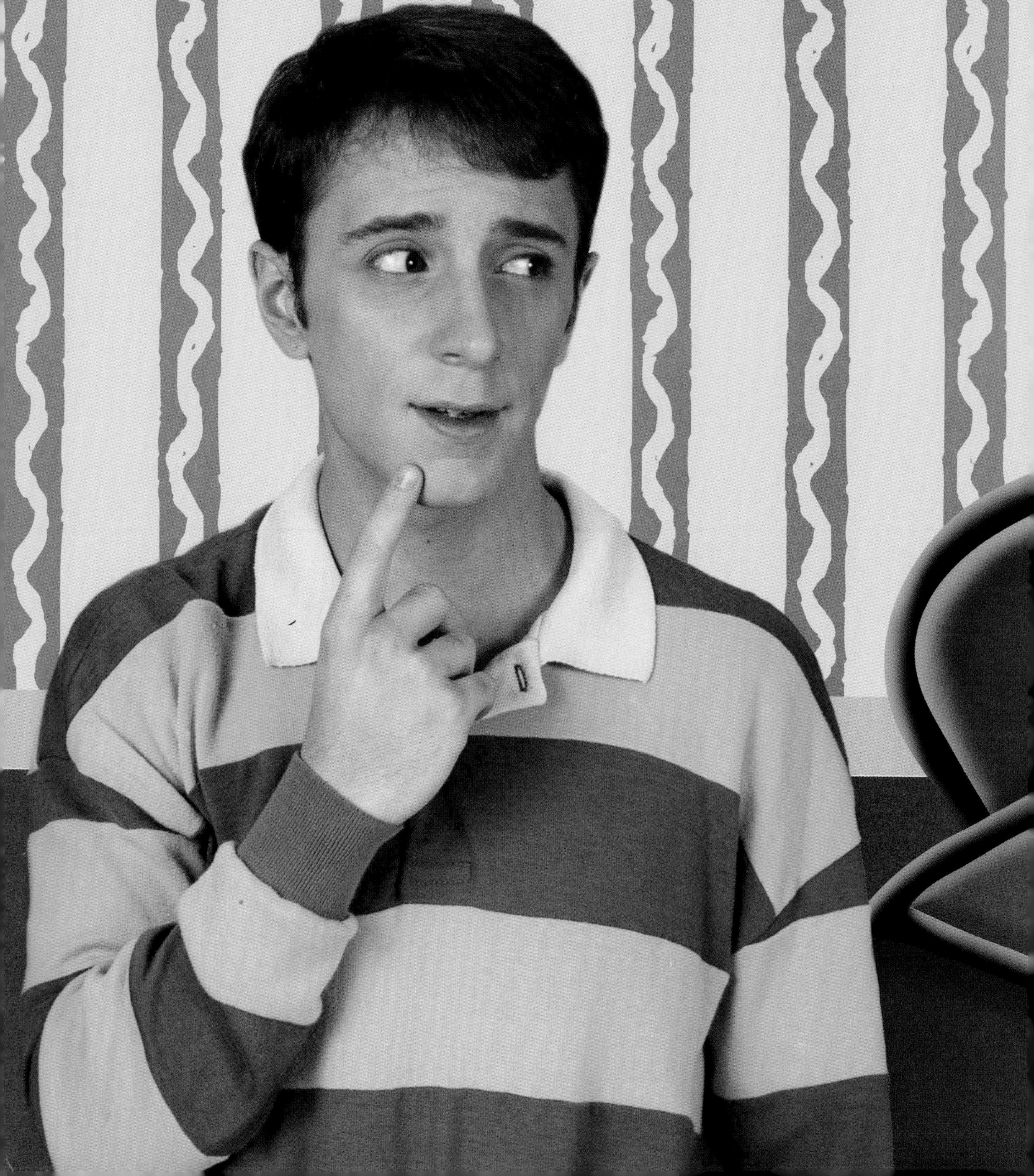

String is our first clue! What do you think Blue wants to do on this windy day with string? Hmmm. We'd better find the other two clues to help us figure this out.

Hey, someone's knocking at the door. Well, let's go see who it is!

Look! Magenta is here for her play date. Come on in. Hurry, Magenta! The wind is blowing everything around.

Will you help us figure out what's not where it belongs? You will? Thanks!

Whew! Thanks for all of your help. We fixed the phone, and we put the blocks back together. Anything else? Oh! The lampshade! Which way did it go? Oh . . . toward the kitchen? Let's go!

We found the lampshade! Good work!

What's that? A clue? The spoons are a clue! Now, what could Blue want to do on a windy day with string and spoons? I don't know about you, but I can't wait to find our last clue!

Look, Blue and Magenta are coloring a picture together. Can you tell what it is?

You see another clue? It's the wind! The wind is our third and last clue! You know what that means? It's time to go to our . . . Thinking Chair!

Hmmm. Spoons blowing in the wind make noise, don't they? Do you want to make a wind chime, Blue? You do? Cool! We just figured out Blue's Clues!

Our wind chime is done and ready to hang. Now we'll have music whenever the wind blows. Thanks so much for your help!

BLUE'S WHIMSICAL WIND CHIME

You will need: string or fishing line, metal teaspoons and tablespoons (4-6 total), and a sturdy stick

1. Ask a grown-up to help you cut a 12-14 inch piece of string for every spoon you'll be using.

2. Tie one end of the string at the base of a spoon handle.

3. Tie the other end of the string around the stick.

4. Repeat steps 2 and 3 with each spoon, making sure that the spoons are close enough together to hit each other easily.

5. Tie one more string to the middle of the stick for hanging the wind chime from a tree branch or other object. Now wait for a windy day!